Looking for Yesterday

*"Happiness, not in another place but this place...
not for another hour, but this hour."*
Walt Whitman

For Mark and Lucy, I hope all your todays
and tomorrows are the best. Love from Alison

AN OLD BARN BOOK

First published in 2017 in the UK and Australia and New Zealand
by Old Barn Books Ltd, Warren Barn, West Sussex, RH20 1JW, UK
www.oldbarnbooks.com

Distributed in the UK by Bounce Sales & Marketing
and in Australia and New Zealand by Walker Books Australia

The illustrations were created using alkyd oil paints

Design by Mike Jolley
Pre-press and Production by Hinotori Media

FIRST EDITION

ISBN 978-1-910646-212

10 9 8 7 6 5 4 3 2 1

Printed in Italy

Looking for Yesterday

Alison Jay

Old Barn Books

Yesterday was the best day.

I wish I could go back and do it all again.

But how?

I know when you look at the stars
you are looking at light from a million yesterdays.

I would need to go faster than light –

One hundred and eighty-six thousand miles per second...

over seven and a half times anti-clockwise

$$V(x) = f^{Ev_0}$$
$$\beta = v/c$$
$$\sqrt{2} E$$

299792458 m/s

around the earth every second...   to get back to yesterday.

What goes faster
than light?

A bus can't travel at superluminal speed.

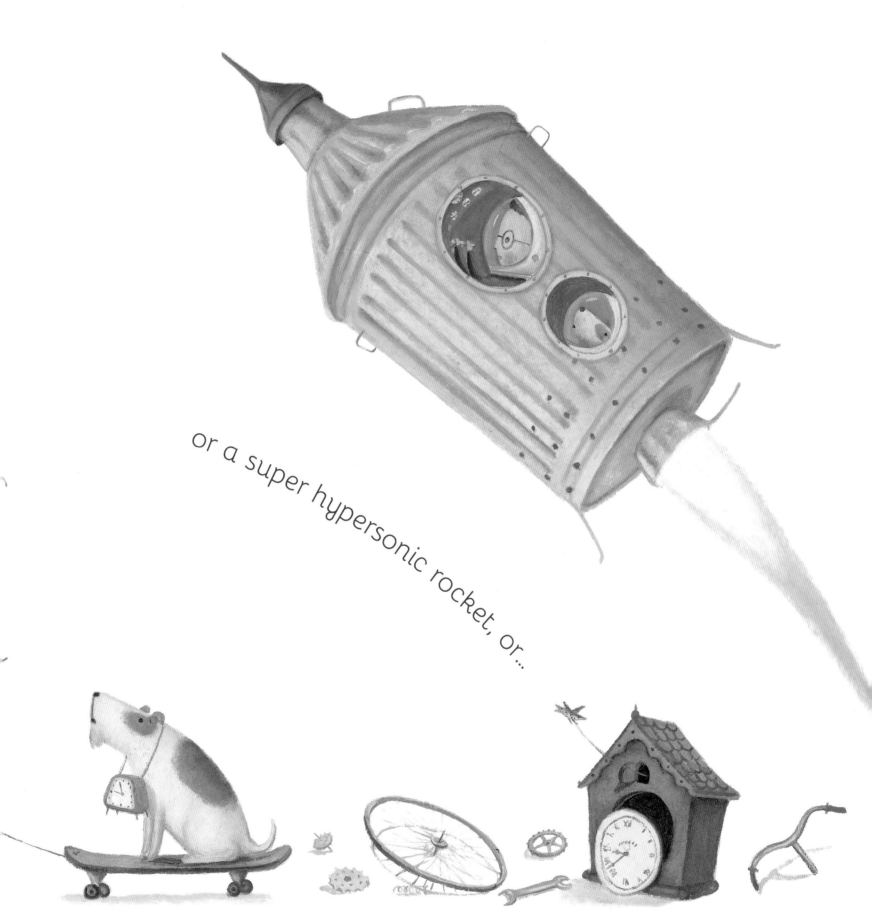

or a super hypersonic rocket, or...

Some scientists say there are wormholes in space that could take us back in time...

I've just got to find one!

(and shrink myself to one billion, trillion, trillionth of a centimetre!)

That's not one...

I don't think this is one...

Grandad, can you
help me to find the way
back to yesterday?

"Why do you want to go back to yesterday?

"Because it was the *best* day Grandad!"

"Yesterday was a wonderful day, but there are many more happy days to come.

Let me tell you about some of my best days."

I have seen ten thousand birds fly through a sunset...

I have seen bright lights shimmer across a black sky...

I have danced by moonlight with the love of my life...

I have laughed until dawn with friends old and new.

and over thundering water.

I have climbed high to the top of a snow-capped mountain...

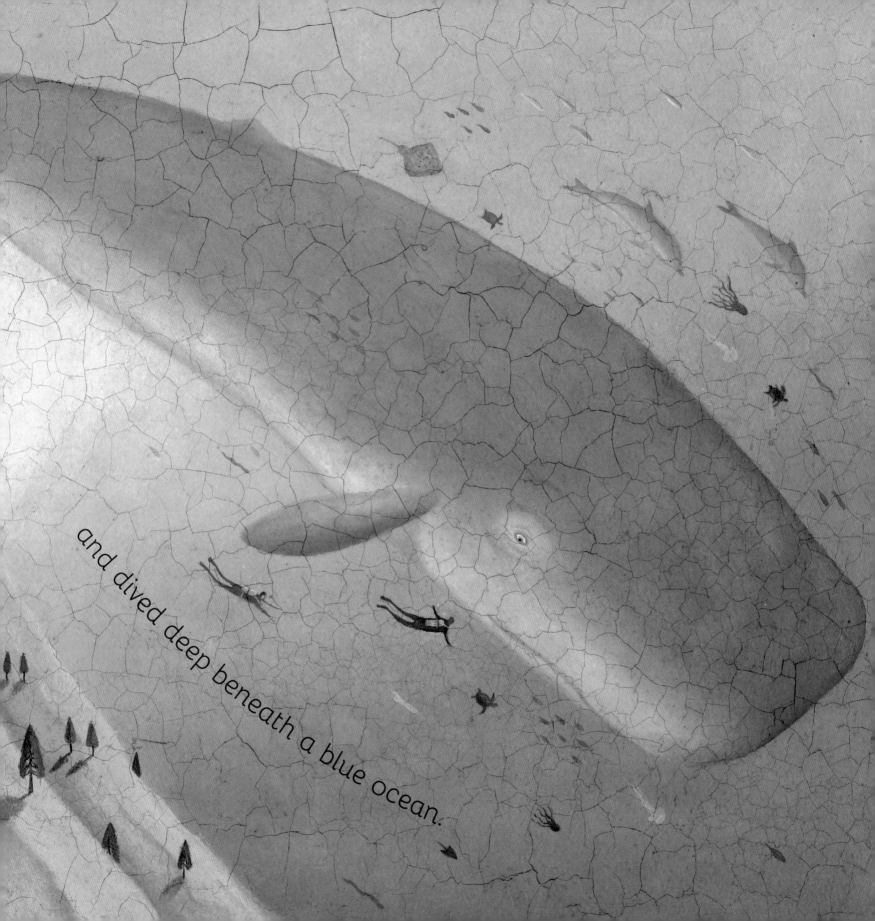

and dived deep beneath a blue ocean.

Our best days make happy memories,

But every day brings the chance of a new adventure.
Why go looking for yesterday when you can be happy here...

TODAY!